LITTLE WOLF
and the
GIANT

SUE PORTER

SIMON AND SCHUSTER BOOKS FOR YOUNG READERS

PUBLISHED BY SIMON & SCHUSTER INC., NEW YORK

FOR BEST FRIENDS – Danny Carla James David Kirsty Tom Megan David

SIMON AND SCHUSTER BOOKS FOR YOUNG READERS
Simon & Schuster Building, Rockefeller Center
1230 Avenue of the Americas, New York, New York 10020
Text copyright © 1989 by Sue Porter
Illustrations copyright © 1989 by Sue Porter
All rights reserved including the right of
reproduction in whole or in part in any form
Originally published in Great Britain by Simon & Schuster Limited.
First U.S. edition 1990
SIMON AND SCHUSTER BOOKS FOR YOUNG READERS
is a trademark of Simon & Schuster Inc.
Manufactured in Belgium

10 9 8 7 6 5 4 3 2 1

Library of Congress Cataloging-in-Publication Data
Porter, Sue.   Little Wolf and the giant.
Summary: Little Wolf's terror at being followed by a
giant in the woods is alleviated when he finds out the
reason for the pursuit. [1. Wolves—Fiction.   2. Giants—
Fiction]   I. Title.
PZ7.P8339Li 1990   [E]   89-21886
ISBN 0-671-70363-3

As Little Wolf was getting ready to visit his Granny, he felt worried. She lived on the other side of a big, spooky woods. "Are there any giants in the woods?" he asked his Mother.

"Of course not, silly," she said.

Little Wolf set off. But he had only gone a short way, when he heard a dreadful noise.

slurp, slurp, slurp.

"I know there aren't any giants," he said aloud. But, just in case, he speeded up and trotted along at a much quicker pace. Suddenly, he saw a great big rock blocking the path. He didn't slow down at all, but sailed right over the top.

CRASH!

"*Aaargh!*" cried the Giant, who
didn't notice the rock until
he tripped over it.

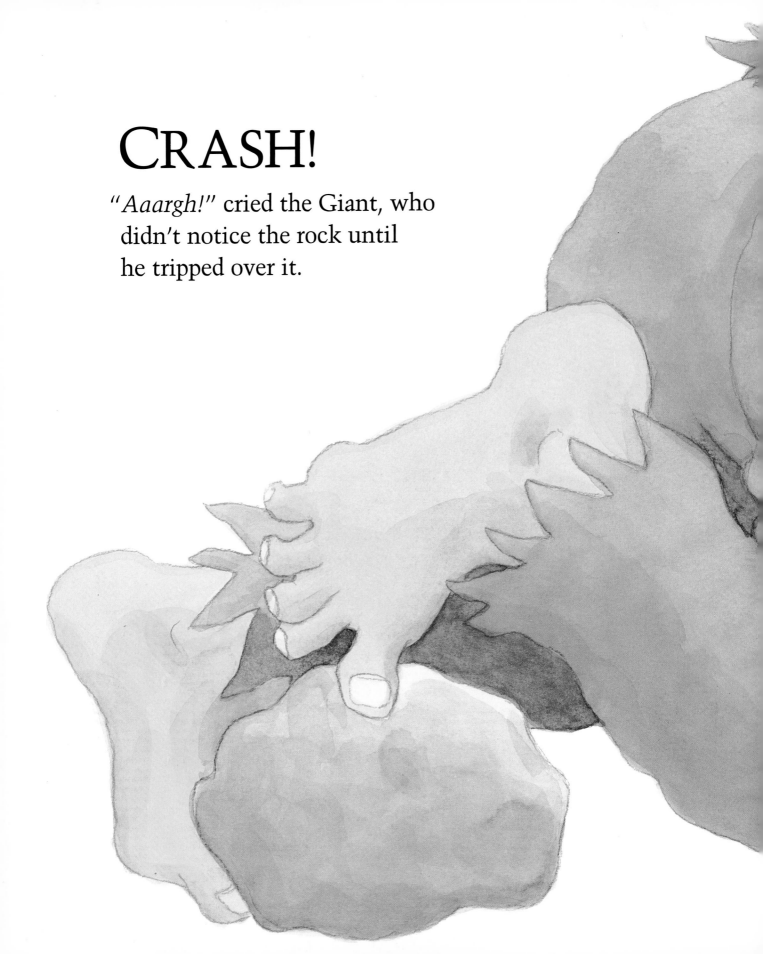

Little Wolf heard the crash. He didn't dare to look. He began to shake and started to run. Suddenly, he saw a great big hole right in his path. He didn't slow down at all, but sailed right over the top.

CRASH!

"Aaargh!" cried the Giant, who didn't notice
the hole until he fell right into it.

"Oh no!" shrieked Little Wolf as he heard the crash. "It *is* a giant!" He forced his legs to run faster. Suddenly, he saw a rickety, old bridge ahead. He didn't slow down at all, but sailed right over the top.

SPLASH!

"Aaargh!" cried the Giant as the rickety, old
bridge broke under his weight.

"Help! Help!" screamed Little Wolf as he
heard the splash close behind him. He
looked over his shoulder instead of where he
was going and didn't see the fallen tree
blocking the path…

CRASH!

"Aaargh!" cried Little Wolf as he tripped and tumbled into the branches. Although he struggled he was trapped. Then, he heard the Giant's footsteps coming closer and closer…

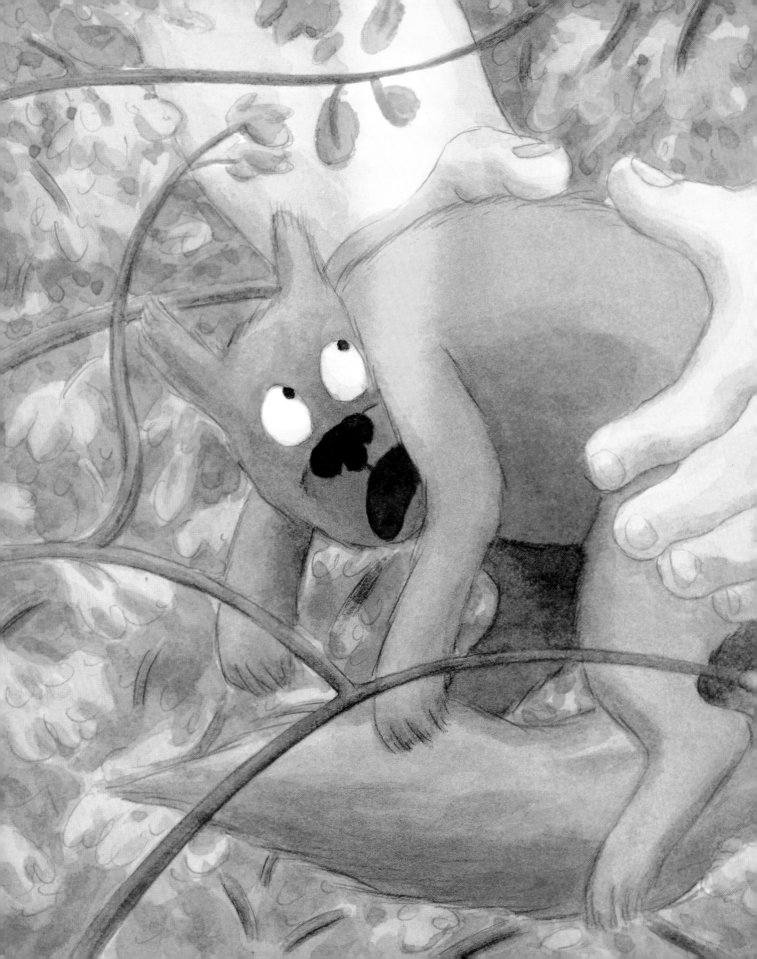

"Save me, save me!" cried Little
Wolf. But it was too late. A huge pair of
hands grabbed him.
"At last," boomed the big voice
of the Giant.

"I've been trying to catch up with you," explained the Giant. "You dropped this cupcake right at the edge of the woods." "Th-thank you," said Little Wolf, who was still a bit scared. "I thought you were after me."

"Everyone always thinks that," said the Giant, sadly. "I don't have any friends, I look so scary."

"I'll be your friend," replied Little Wolf. "Come and have tea at Granny's with me."

"Yes *please*," said the Giant. "I'm so glad you're not scared of giants anymore."

"But I am scared of witches," said Little Wolf. "Do you think there are any witches in the woods?"

"Of course not, silly," said the Giant.
And off they set.